Things to RACE CARS

By Craig Robert Carey

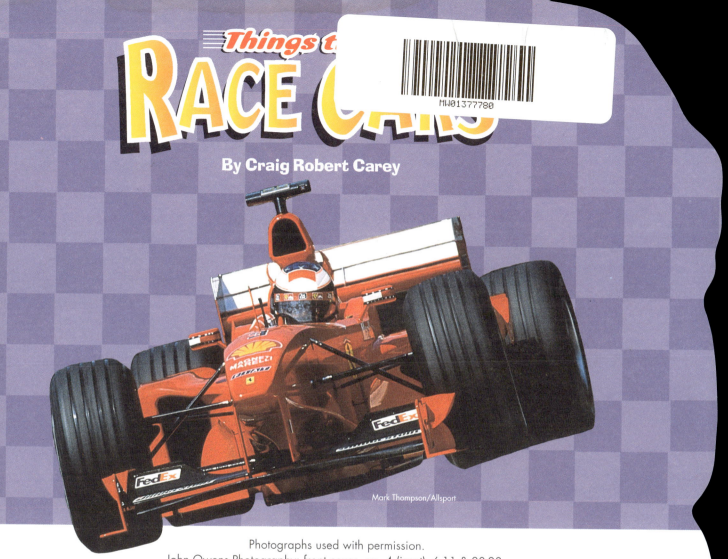

Mark Thompson/Allsport

Photographs used with permission.
John Owens Photography: front cover, pp. 4 (inset), 6-11 & 20-23.
Allsport: back cover, pp.1-5, 10 (inset), 12-19 & 20 (insets).
Index Stock Imagery: pp. 7 (inset) & 24.

 A GOLDEN BOOK • NEW YORK

Golden Books Publishing Company, Inc., New York, New York 10106

© 2001 Golden Books Publishing Company, Inc. All rights reserved. Printed in the U.S.A. No part of this book may be reproduced or copied in any form without written permission from the copyright owner. GOLDEN BOOKS®, A GOLDEN BOOK®, G DESIGN®, and the distinctive spine are registered trademarks of Golden Books Publishing Company, Inc. Library of Congress Catalog Card Number: 00-106767   ISBN: 0-307-10344-7   A MMI First Edition 2001
10 9 8 7 6 5 4 3 2 1

ZOOM!

Pascal Rondeau/Allsport

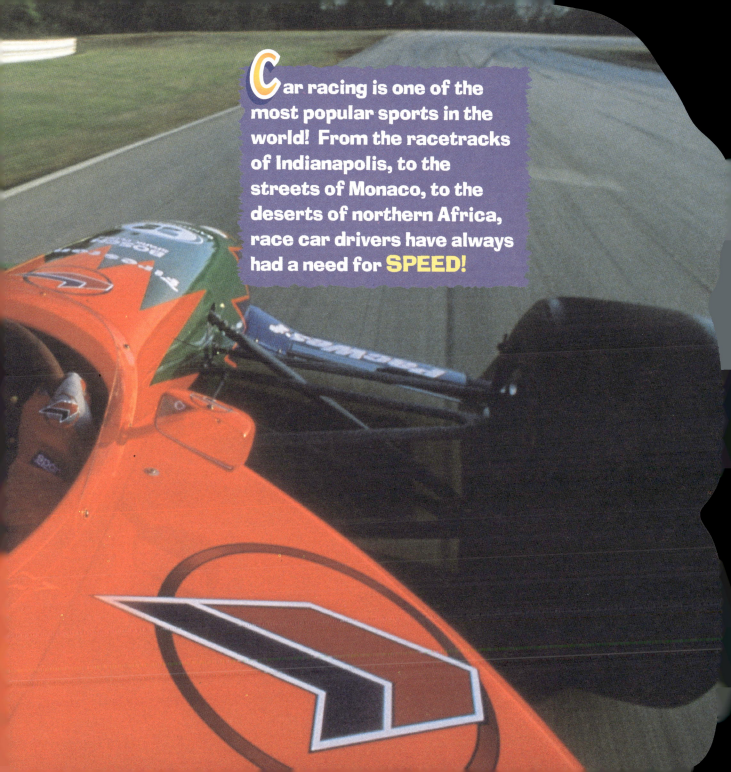

Car racing is one of the most popular sports in the world! From the racetracks of Indianapolis, to the streets of Monaco, to the deserts of northern Africa, race car drivers have always had a need for **SPEED!**

Car racing has been around almost as long as cars have—over 100 years! The first major racing events included the 24-hour **LE MANS** race and the **GRAND PRIX** races in Europe. Now car races are held all over the world.

John Owens Photography

Bernard Asset/Allsport

The first race cars were just regular cars with a few special changes—like a more powerful engine—to make them go faster.

Today, almost all race cars are designed specifically for a certain kind of race and even a certain kind of track. They're built to **WIN!**

John Owens Photography

SCREECH!

Benelux Press/Index Stock Imagery

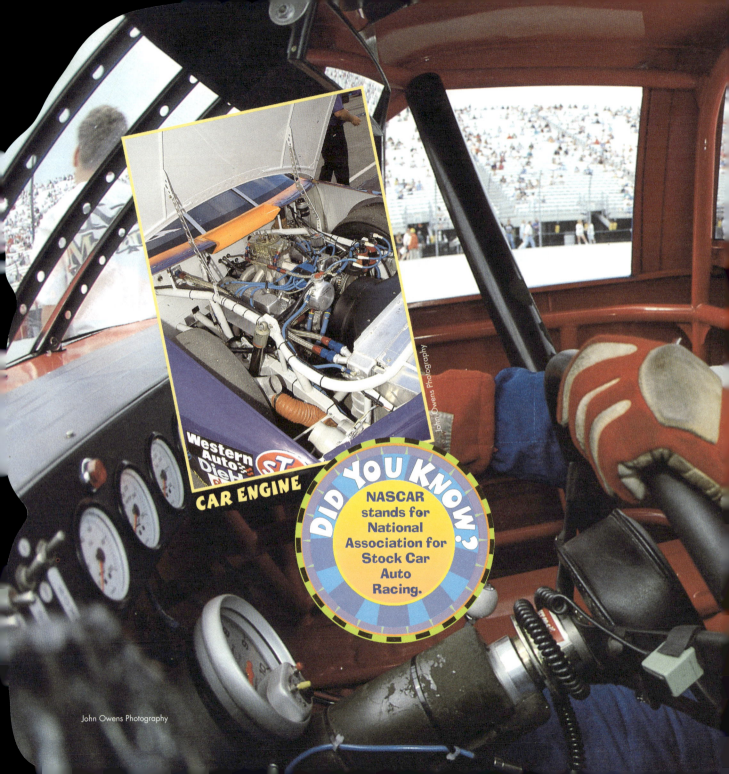

Western
Auto
Diehl

CAR ENGINE

John Owens Photography

John Owens Photography

DID YOU KNOW?

NASCAR stands for National Association for Stock Car Auto Racing.

STOCK **CARS** are the most popular race cars in America. They may look like regular cars, but don't let that fool you. Every part, from the engine to the tires, is specially built!

John Owens Photography

Craig Jones/Allsport

RICHARD PETTY

DID YOU KNOW?

Richard Petty has won more NASCAR races than any other driver! He's helped make the sport as popular as it is.

John Owens Photography

STOCK CARS race close together at high speeds, often bumping into one another. The drivers have to be very skillful!

Steve Swope/Allsport

MARIO ANDRETTI

DID YOU KNOW?

Mario Andretti may be the greatest race car driver ever! He's best known for driving Formula One cars.

Michael Cooper/Allsport

Another type of race car is the **FORMULA ONE.** Formula One cars are very streamlined and can go as fast as 200 miles per hour!

The most famous Formula One race is the **MONACO GRAND PRIX.** (Grand Prix means "big prize" in French.) Instead of circling around a race track, the race weaves its way through city streets and highways!

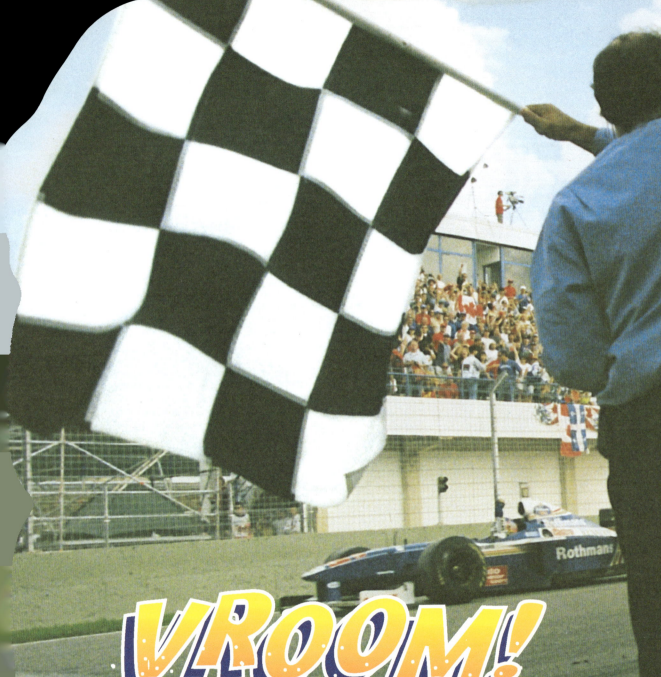

VROOM!

Mark Thompson/Allsport

INDY CARS are a lot like Formula Ones, but they're even more powerful! The **INDIANAPOLIS 500** is one of the longest races. The track is only two and a half miles long, so the drivers have to go around it 200 times to complete the 500-mile race!

DID YOU KNOW?

The Indianapolis Speedway is also called "The Brickyard," because for years the track was made of bricks!

Ken Levine/Allsport

DRAGSTERS are the fastest race cars in the world, but they race the shortest distance. DRAG RACES are over in seconds!

The cars have huge rear wheels and superpowerful engines. They race down the track at over 320 miles an hour!

DID YOU KNOW?

Dragsters use a parachute at the end of a race to help them slow down.

PARIS TO DAKAR RALLY

Vandystadt/Allsport

Vandystadt/Allsport

Some race cars and trucks are specially built to speed over dirt and rocks, dodging boulders and other obstacles. That's what **OFF-ROAD RACING** is all about. It's a rough ride!

The most famous off-road race is the **PARIS TO DAKAR RALLY** that goes through France and northern Africa. Competitors drive through mountains and deserts in a race that lasts for weeks!

ROLLIN'!

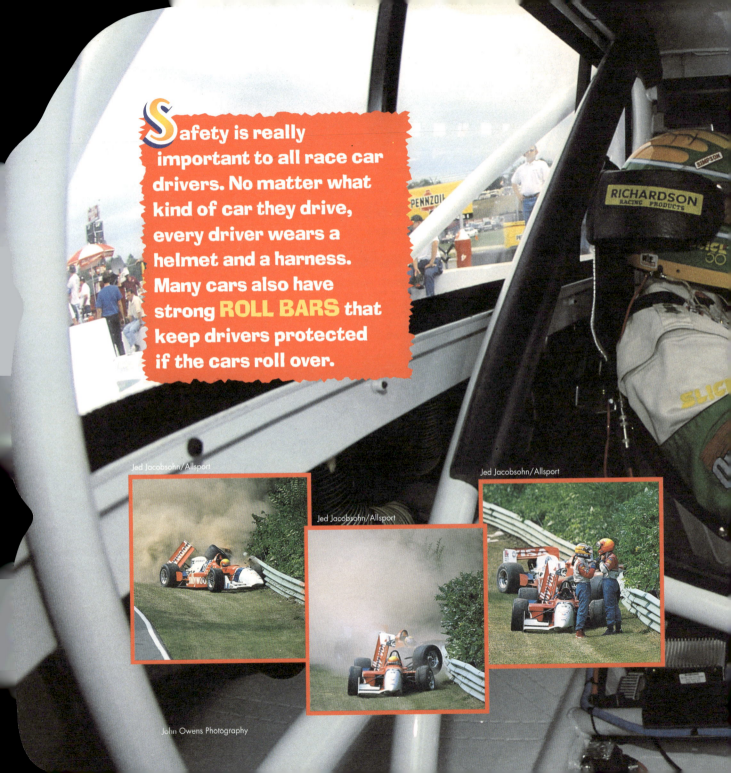

Safety is really important to all race car drivers. No matter what kind of car they drive, every driver wears a helmet and a harness. Many cars also have strong **ROLL BARS** that keep drivers protected if the cars roll over.

Jed Jacobsohn/Allsport

Jed Jacobsohn/Allsport

Jed Jacobsohn/Allsport

John Owens Photography

DID YOU KNOW?
Fire trucks and ambulances are always standing by in case of a crash.

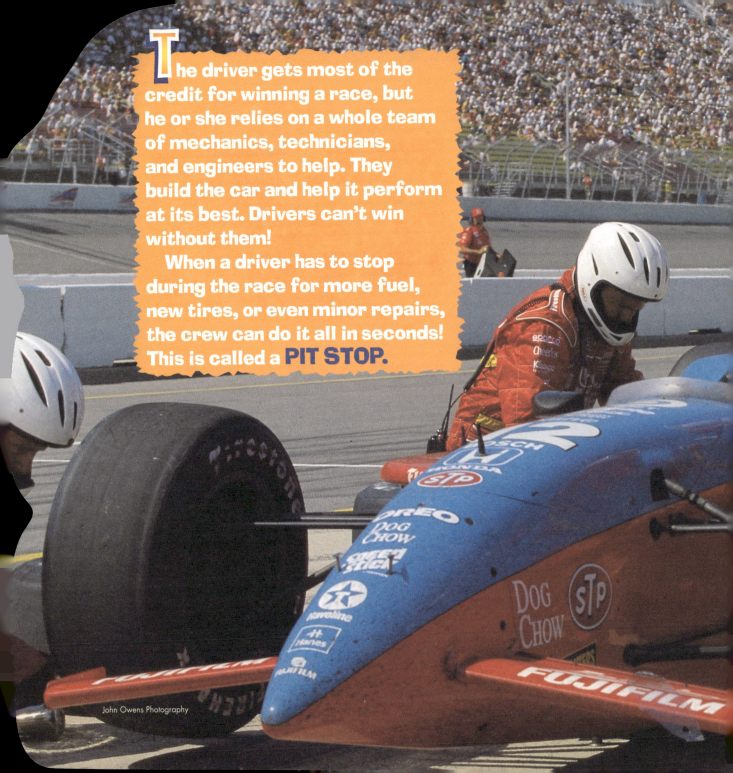

The driver gets most of the credit for winning a race, but he or she relies on a whole team of mechanics, technicians, and engineers to help. They build the car and help it perform at its best. Drivers can't win without them!

When a driver has to stop during the race for more fuel, new tires, or even minor repairs, the crew can do it all in seconds! This is called a **PIT STOP.**

John Owens Photography

Car racing is one of the hottest sports around, and it just keeps getting hotter!

WANT TO LEARN MORE?
Check out these Web sites:
www.nascar.com
www.formula1.com
www.indyracingleague.com
www.nhra.com

Zefa/Index Stock Imagery